U0015288

BOOK

OF

LOVE

愛恨，鏡像雙生的情感

毛姆／雨果／珍・奧斯汀——等人合著

王凌緯——譯

目次

愛恨，人生的美好缺憾

告別漫漫黑夜，睜開雙眼，下了床衣著整齊，把視線從天花板轉移到報紙上。一直以來習慣把咖啡當成孤獨的處方，晨間音樂使人放鬆，之後再將一天揮灑得匆忙，生活一切恍如夢境。然而在這尋常不過的場景，多數人或許不會注意到，那悄悄佔據一方的人類情感。情歌總在榜上，人與人之關係早已是陳腔濫調，每日收錄在副刊及專欄，歷久不衰。就連一本正經的電影也總要使些愛恨情仇，好似無此調味便難以下嚥。

愛情。有人看得入迷，有人嗤之以鼻，但無論如何，面對這如詛咒般的天性，人註定是無路可逃。

也許人第一次意識到愛的存在，是親情 —— 兒時受呵護的滿足，又或者和親人別離的深刻記憶。打那時起，這種情感彷若仙氣，自神燈中蔓延而出，

在人眼前蒙上了一幕刷洗不去的印象。

　　情感的發源正如雛鳥的印記行為，一旦認定、成形，便化身狂熱分子。對人而言，雖然投射對象不是親鳥，且凡事各有造化，但人總能使自己在世間角落陷入癡迷。這似乎是種天性，一片汪洋中找尋光芒，即使那對象微不足道——

　　他端望窗前透光的植栽，細細品味生命的消長；他飼養過寵物，但曾經的生離死別如今教他不敢造次；物質生活與便利的引力，絲毫比不上他對居所與故土的鄉愁；他對自己念舊的性格十分無助，當整理房間看見一抽屜的過去，每每感到陌生而熟悉。

　　不單單如此，感情還有更濃烈的可能。

　　愛的基因中藏有毀滅，毀滅的盡頭也埋伏著愛。某些時候，人即使深愛某物，同時卻偏偏無可自拔地傷害它；而恨的隱義則是珍惜，當一個人恨得無可救藥，最後卻彷彿吸毒，只能與它的成癮性苟且共生——

　　那麼一隻寄生在宿主身上的生物，他對宿主究竟是愛，抑或恨呢？他心底當然愛死這衣食父母了，情不自禁地依賴，但誰能想到自己情感如此不潔？浮沉於矛盾間，他的依存，啃咬宿主的肉時又該抱著何種心情？接下來，他唯有小心翼翼地維繫彼此

生命，直到一方停止心跳。

也許那般諸多複雜的情感，起源皆相同，發跡在造物主造人之時，無意間錯寫的一行程式碼。它過於柔情，對象不定，它面貌多變，宛若千面女郎。然而愛的亙古之謎，這個被無數人研究過無數次的問題，歷經了千年依然沒有解答。

縱使煞費苦心，從無人敢稱自己「已經明白愛為何物」，就像是沒有科學家敢說自己掌握了宇宙真理，即便如此，欲靠近真理只得放手追尋。

《愛恨，鏡像雙生的情感》收錄一百四十多則名篇佳句，是逾五十位名家的獨到領略。他們各有故事，體悟非凡而深刻，讓讀者透過這些字句一窺他們為自己獨白的各種表情。

首章〈幻想之預示〉述說著一種期待，是對於未知旅途的行前說明。很快地，當踏入了一段關係，幸福和喜悅匆匆佔據內心，二章〈愛中飛翔〉道出了這般讓人忘卻現實的甜膩滋味，就在這段時光，飛蛾撲火變成了一種讚許。但接踵而來的是夢魘，卻多少人甘願被蒙住雙眼，不願離開樂園。三章〈幸福的海市蜃樓〉中，曾經的甘美攤開在那呼之欲出

的全貌上，就將回憶作為覺醒之代價。最後不論是否處於關係內，人終究得起身，此時此刻，想法已超脫關係本身。

終章〈如夢初醒〉描繪那雨後的虹光，清晰分明地向人發送美好。也許曾酣暢一場，或盜汗一陣，乍時，旅人已收拾好思緒，雲淡風輕。

由這些名家精美的文字引領，我們一同踏上天馬行空的愛恨奇想。任憑將至的酸甜苦辣，字裡行間就是地圖，曾經的故事則是指南，為黑夜打底——

眼前，那是一道嶄新的關口。

無論穿越與否，行者終將整備好心情動身，自此之後，忘卻了失眠的顏色，如夢初醒。

I

幻想之預示

Love is a serious mental disease.

────**Plato** 427-347 BC : *Phaedrus*

愛是一種嚴重的心理殘疾。

—— 柏拉圖《斐多篇》

Perhaps all the dragons in our lives are princesses who are only waiting to see us act, just once, with beauty and courage. Perhaps everything that frightens us is, in its deepest essence, something helpless that wants our love.

——**Rainer Maria Rilke** 1875-1926 : *Letters to a Young Poet*

也許我們生命中的惡龍，是那些等著看我們以美與勇氣犯難的公主 —— 就只看那麼一次。也許所有教我們害怕的事物，在其本質深處都無助地索求著我們的愛。

—— **里爾克**《致年輕詩人的信》

If you love deeply, you're going to get hurt badly. But it's still worth it.

——**C.S. Lewis** 1898-1963 : *Shadowlands*

如果你愛得太深，你會重傷。但那仍然值得。

—— C.S. 路易士《影子大地》

The power of a glance has been so much abused in love stories, that it has come to be disbelieved in. Few people dare now to say that two beings have fallen in love because they have looked at each other. Yet it is in this way that love begins, and in this way only.

——**Victor Hugo** 1802-1885 : *Les Misérables*

眼神的力量在愛情故事中早已變作陳腔濫調，不足
採信。鮮少有人敢再宣稱，只消一次四目相接便能
使兩人相愛。然而這卻是所有愛情開始的方式，也
是唯一的方式。

──雨果《悲慘世界》

愛恨，鏡像雙生的情感

19

It is wrong to think that love comes from long companionship and persevering courtship. Love is the offspring of spiritual affinity and unless that affinity is created in a moment, it will not be created for years or even generations.

——**Kahlil Gibran** 1883-1931 : *The Broken Wings*

以為愛來自長久相處與堅定追求是錯的。愛是靈性吸引的產物，而那種吸引力生成於一瞬之間，而非來自數年、甚至數個世代的努力。

—— 紀伯倫《斷翼》

And now here is my secret, a very simple secret: It is only with the heart that one can see rightly; what is essential is invisible to the eye.

———**Antoine de Saint-Exupéry** 1900-1944 : *The Little Prince*

愛恨，鏡像雙生的情感

我的祕密在此。相當簡單：用心看得比眼睛還多。
本質是眼睛看不見的。

—— 聖修伯里《小王子》

How we need another soul to cling to, another body to keep us warm. To rest and trust; to give your soul in confidence: I need this, I need someone to pour myself into.

———**Sylvia Plath** 1932-1963 : *The Unabridged Journals of Sylvia Plath*

我們多麼需要另一個靈魂來倚靠、另一具肉體以取
暖。歇息、信任；篤定地給出你的靈魂：我需要，
我需要一個能讓我傾注自身的人。

──雪維亞・普拉絲《普拉絲日誌》

Selfishness is one of the qualities apt to inspire love.

——**Nathaniel Hawthorne** 1804-1864 : *American Notebooks*

自私是容易啟發愛的特質之一。

—— 納撒尼爾 · 霍桑《美國散記》

Love is always open arms. If you close your arms about love you will find that you are left holding only yourself.

——**Leo Buscaglia** 1924-1998 : *Love*

愛恨，鏡像雙生的情感

愛總是敞開雙臂。如果你對愛闔上雙臂，你會發現
自己只被自己環抱。

── 利奧‧巴士卡力《愛》

Nobody dies from lack of sex. It's lack of love we die from.

——**Margaret Atwood** 1939- : *The Handmaid's Tale*

沒有人會因床事匱乏而死。我們會死於愛情匱乏。

——瑪格麗特・艾特伍《使女的故事》

Never close your lips to those whom you have already
opened your heart.

——**Charles Dickens** 1812-1870

別對那些你已敞開心房的人緊閉雙唇。

──狄更斯

It is the time you have wasted for your rose that makes your rose so important.

——**Antoine de Saint-Exupéry** 1900-1944 : *The Little Prince*

愛恨，鏡像雙生的情感

是你耗費在你玫瑰上的時間使她變得如此重要。

—— 聖修伯里《小王子》

Gravitation is not responsible for people falling in
love.

——**Albert Einstein** 1879-1955

人墮入情網並非萬有引力之故。

──愛因斯坦

I think... if it is true that there are as many minds as there are heads, then there are as many kinds of love as there are hearts.

——**Leo Tolstoy** 1828-1910 : *Anna Karenina*

我想……若有多少個腦子裝有多少種心靈，那麼就有多少顆心夾著多少種愛情。

—— **托爾斯泰**《安娜·卡列尼娜》

People should fall in love with their eyes closed.

——**Andy Warhol** 1928-1987

愛恨，鏡像雙生的情感

墮入愛河時人們都該閉上眼睛。

──安迪・沃荷

The meeting of two personalities is like the contact of two chemical substances: if there is any reaction, both are transformed.

——**Carl Jung** 1875-1961 : *Modern Man in Search of a Soul*

兩個人格的相遇就像兩種化學物質接觸：如果當中有任何反應，那兩方都會有所變化。

—— **榮格** 《尋求靈魂的現代人》

Pleasure in this respect is like photography. What we take, in the presence of the beloved object, is merely a negative film, which we develop later, when we are back at home, and have once again found at our disposal that inner darkroom the entrance to which is barred to us so long as we are with other people.

——**Marcel Proust** 1871-1922 : *Within a Budding Grove*

有種快樂如同攝影術。心愛對象在場時，我們能得到的僅僅是一張底片，這張底片要在我們稍後回到家中，親自使用內心的暗房才能沖洗出來，如此回味這種快樂。而只要有旁人，這間暗房的入口便會闔上。

—— **普魯斯特**《在少女們身旁》

The whole world is divided for me into two parts: one is she, and there is all happiness, hope, light; the other is where she is not, and there is dejection and darkness...

——**Leo Tolstoy** 1828-1910 : *War and Peace*

愛恨，鏡像雙生的情感

整個世界對我而言分成兩半：一半是她，在那裡有一切幸福、希望與光；另一半是她不在之處，那裡只有沮喪與黑暗……

——**托爾斯泰**《戰爭與和平》

To be together is for us to be at once as free as in solitude, as gay as in company. We talk, I believe, all day long; to talk to each other is but a more animated and an audible thinking.

——**Charlotte Bronte** 1816-1855 : *Jane Eyre*

對我們而言，相聚也有如獨處般自由，如友伴般快活。我相信我們能聊上整天；我們的交談不過就是一種更加生動而聽得見的思緒。

——夏綠蒂‧勃朗特《簡愛》

愛恨，鏡像雙生的情感

It was a very very nice letter you wrote by the light
of the stars at midnight. Always write then, for your
heart requires moonlight to deliquesce it.

———**Virginia Woolf** 1882-1941 : *letter to Vita Sackville-West*

你在午夜星光下寫來的信相當相當好。總在那時寫信，因為你的心需要月光照拂才能溶解。

—— 吳爾芙，致友人薇塔的信

If I had a flower for every time I thought of you...I could walk through my garden forever.

——**Alfred Tennyson** 1809-1892 : *Queen Mary*

若想你一次能讓一朵花綻放，我將永遠無法步出我
的花園。

—— 丁尼生 《瑪麗皇后》

Being with you and not being with you is the only way
I have to measure time.

——**Jorge Luis Borges** 1899-1986 : *The Threatened One*

我測量時間的唯一方式，是與你同在，或不。

── 波赫士《受威脅者》

Lolita, light of my life, fire of my loins. My sin, my soul. Lo-lee-ta: the tip of the tongue taking a trip of three steps. Down the palate to tap, at three, on the teeth. Lo. Lee. Ta.

——**Vladimir Nabokov** 1899-1977 : *Lolita*

蘿莉塔，我生命的幽光、我腰胯的熱火。我的罪惡、我的靈魂。蘿－莉－塔：舌尖小跳三步，沿著上顎一路下探，第三步於齒面上輕彈。蘿。莉。塔。

──納博科夫《蘿莉塔》

A lady's imagination is very rapid; it jumps from admiration to love, from love to matrimony in a moment.

———Jane Austen 1775-1817 : *Pride and Prejudice*

愛恨，鏡像雙生的情感

女士的想像力一日能行千里；僅僅一瞬之間，好感遂躍升為愛情、愛情更躍升為婚姻。

—— 珍・奧斯汀《傲慢與偏見》

No thorns go as deep as a rose's,
And love is more cruel than lust.

——**Algernon Charles Swinburne** 1837-1909 : *'Dolores'*

沒有荊棘比玫瑰刺得更深，
而愛情遠比色慾來得殘酷。

—— 史雲朋〈憂愁〉

The most painful thing is losing yourself in the process of loving someone too much, and forgetting that you are special too.

——**Ernest Hemingway** 1899-1961 : *Men Without Women*

愛恨，鏡像雙生的情感

世間最痛苦莫過於愛一個人太深而迷失自己，迷失
到你忘了自己同樣特別。

—— 海明威《沒有女人的男人》

There are the lover and the beloved, but these two come from different countries.

——**Carson McCullers** 1917-1967 : *Ballad of the Sad Café*

愛恨，鏡像雙生的情感

世上有人愛人、有人被愛，但這兩種人來自不同國
度。

——卡森・麥卡勒斯《傷心咖啡館之歌》

Is that a gun in your pocket, or are you just glad to see me?

——**Mae West** 1893-1980 : *Peel Me a Grape*

你口袋裡那是一把槍呢，還是單純看到我很開心？

—— **梅・蕙絲** 《給我剝顆葡萄》

In love there is always one who kisses and one who offers the cheek.

——**French proverb**

在愛情裡總是有一個人獻上親吻、一個人湊上臉頰。

── 法國俚語

When someone blushes, doesn't that mean 'yes'?

——**Antoine de Saint-Exupéry** 1900-1944 : *The Little Prince*

愛恨，鏡像雙生的情感

當一個人開始臉紅，難道不就是在說「我願意」嗎？

—— 聖修伯里《小王子》

A kiss can be a comma, a question mark or an exclamation point. That's basic spelling that every woman ought to know.

——**Mistinguette** 1875-1956 : *Theater Arts*

爱恨，鏡像雙生的情感

一個吻能是一個逗點、一個問號或一個驚嘆號。這
是每個女人都該知道的基本拼寫。

—— 蜜絲婷瑰《論劇場藝術》

Talk to every woman as if you loved her, and to every man as if he bored you, and at the end of your first season you will have the reputation of possessing the most perfect social tact.

——**Oscar Wilde** 1854-1900 : *A Woman of No Importance*

對每個女人說話，說得好像你深愛著她，對每個男人說話，說得好像他使你厭倦，然後在第一季結束前，你臻至完美的社交手腕就會聲名鵲起。

—— 王爾德《無足輕重的女人》

The magic of first love is our ignotance that it can ever end.

——**Benjamin Disraeli** 1804-1881 : *Henriette Temple*

初戀的魔力源於無知，無知於初戀竟有可能結束。

—— 班傑明·迪斯雷利 《亨利埃塔·坦普爾》

Never love anyone who treats you like you're ordinary.

———**Oscar Wilde** 1854-1900

千萬別愛上把你當一般人看待的人。

—— 王爾德

愛恨，鏡像雙生的情感

BOOK OF LOVE

II

愛中飛翔

Every heart sings a song, incomplete, until another heart whispers back. Those who wish to sing always find a song. At the touch of a lover, everyone becomes a poet.

——**Plato** 427-347 BC

每顆心都唱著不完整的歌，直到其他心悄聲應和。
願意唱的人永遠找得到一首歌。在愛人的撫觸之下，
所有人都成為詩人。

── 柏拉圖

Love does not consist of gazing at each other, but in looking outward together in the same direction.

——**Antoine de Saint-Exupéry** 1900-1944 : *Airman's Odyssey*

愛恨，鏡像雙生的情感

愛不在於凝視彼此，而在於一起展望相同的方向。

—— 聖修伯里《飛行員的奇幻歷險》

愛恨，鏡像雙生的情感

BOOK OF LOVE

Let there be spaces in your togetherness, And let the winds of the heavens dance between you. Love one another but make not a bond of love: Let it rather be a moving sea between the shores of your souls. Fill each other's cup but drink not from one cup. Give one another of your bread but eat not from the same loaf. Sing and dance together and be joyous, but let each one of you be alone, Even as the strings of a lute are alone though they quiver with the same music. Give your hearts, but not into each other's keeping. For only the hand of Life can contain your hearts. And stand together, yet not too near together: For the pillars of the temple stand apart, And the oak tree and the cypress grow not in each other's shadow.

——**Kahlil Gibran** 1883-1931 : *The Prophet*

為你們的同在挪出空間，讓天堂的風在你們之間拂舞。愛彼此，但不讓愛成為束縛：讓愛成為你們靈魂兩岸之間一片游移的海。斟滿彼此的杯，但不共一杯飲。將你的麵包分予對方而不共一條食。一同歌舞、一同歡樂，但讓你們彼此獨處，如同魯特琴弦儘管共奏一曲，仍然各自獨立。給出你的心，但並非繳給對方看管。只有生命之手能容納你們的心。一同站立，然而別靠太近：寺殿的柱石兀自獨立，而橡木與柏樹並不在彼此遮蔭下茁壯。

—— 紀伯倫《先知》

He had discovered that the time he had in the train going to work was the only time a married man ever go to himself.

——**Katharine Whitehorn** 1928- : *Roundabout*

他發現，在火車上通勤的時間是已婚男子唯一能與
自己相處的時間。

—— 凱瑟琳・懷特霍恩 《拐彎抹角》

We need in love to practice only this:
Letting each other go. For holding on
comes easily; we do not need to learn it.

——**Rainer Maria Rilke** 1875-1926 : *'Requiem for a Friend'*

在愛中，只有此事須加揣摩：

讓彼此好走。因為緊抓不捨

如此自然而然，我們毋庸多學。

—— **里爾克** 〈致友人的安魂曲〉

Love is a striking example of how little reality means
to us.

——**Marcel Proust** 1871-1922 : *À La Recherche du Temps Perdu*

愛是現實對我們而言無關緊要的顯著例證。

—— 普魯斯特《追憶似水年華》

When a woman gets married it is like jumping into a hole in the ice in the middle of winter; you do it once and you remember it the rest of your days.

——**Maxim Gorky** 1868-1936 : *The Lower Depths*

愛恨，鏡像雙生的情感

女人出嫁就像是跳進隆冬裡的冰洞中；你一生就跳
那麼一次，但整個下半輩子都會記得。

──馬克西姆‧高爾基《深淵》

It has made me better loving you... it has made me wiser, and easier, and brighter. I used to want a great many things before, and to be angry that I did not have them. Theoretically, I was satisfied. I flattered myself that I had limited my wants. But I was subject to irritation; I used to have morbid sterile hateful fits of hunger, of desire. Now I really am satisfied, because I can't think of anything better. It's just as when one has been trying to spell out a book in the twilight, and suddenly the lamp comes in. I had been putting out my eyes over the book of life, and finding nothing to reward me for my pains; but now that I can read it properly I see that it's a delightful story.

——**Henry James** 1843-1916 : *The Portrait of a Lady*

愛上你讓我變成更好的人……我變得更睿智、更隨性、更開朗。之前，我總想擁有世間萬物，並為了自己的一無所有而憤怒。理論上我被滿足了。我說服自己早已縮限了自己的欲求。但我仍然受制於惱怒。我曾有源於飢渴和欲求，病態而無謂的恨。但我現在真心知足，因為我已經想像不到其他更好的可能。那就像是有人想在微光中摸索書中的每個字，突然間一盞燈照了下來。此前我已經把眼睛黏到這本生命之書上，卻遍尋不著任何對痛苦的慰藉；但現在我能妥當地閱讀這本書，而且讀出一個令人愉悅的故事。

—— 亨利・詹姆士《仕女圖》

It ought to make us feel ashamed when we talk like
we know what we're talking about when we talk about
love.

——**Raymond Carver** 1938-1988 : *What We Talk When We Talk*
About Love

愛恨，鏡像雙生的情感

當我們談論愛，談論得好像我們自己知道自己在說什麼一樣，這本該是件可恥的事。

—— 瑞蒙・卡佛 《當我們討論愛情》

What is a kiss? Why this, as some approve:
The sure, sweet cement, glue and lime of love.

—— **Robert Herrick** 1591-1674 : *'Kiss'*

愛恨，鏡像雙生的情感

吻為何物？為何這般，如同某些人言之鑿鑿：
是彌封愛的水泥、漿糊與鉚釘，篤實而甜美。

──羅伯‧海瑞克〈吻〉

Sex is an emotion in motion.

──**Mae West** 1893-1980 : *Show*

性是以動作表達的情緒。

　　──梅・蕙絲《秀》

Love has no other desire but to fulfill itself. But if you love and must needs have desires, let these be your desires: To melt and be like a running brook that sings its melody to the night. To know the pain of too much tenderness. To be wounded by your own understanding of love; And to bleed willingly and joyfully. To wake at dawn with a winged heart and give thanks for another day of loving; To rest at noon hour and meditate love's ecstasy; To return home at eventide with gratitude; And then to sleep with a prayer for the beloved in your heart and a song of praise on your lips.

——**Kahlil Gibran** 1883-1931 : *The Prophet*

愛除了實現自身，別無所欲。但你若有愛，則必有所求，就讓這些成為你心所欲：融化，如一道小溪向夜色傾訴衷曲。去認識過多的溫柔帶來的痛苦。為了你對愛的獨到理解遍體鱗傷；然而讓那血流得情願而歡喜。在早晨懷著雀躍之心醒來，感謝又有一日能愛；在午時歇息，沉思愛的狂喜；在昏黃時返家，心滿意足；終而入睡，在你心中為愛人祈禱，唇上輕響讚歌。

—— 紀伯倫《先知》

The more serious the face, the more beautiful the smile.

——**François-René Chateaubriand** 1768-1848 : *Mémoires d'Outre-Tombe*

相敬的臉孔越認真，相愛的微笑越美麗。

—— 夏特布里昂 《墓中回憶錄》

No human relation gives one possession in another—
every two souls are absolutely different. In friendship
or in love, the two side by side raise hands together to
find what one cannot reach alone.

———**Kahlil Gibran** 1883-1931 : *Beloved Prophet: The Love Letters of*
Kahlil Gibran and Mary Haskell, and Her Private Journal

沒有任何人類關係能讓一個人將另一個人據為己有——任兩個靈魂都是截然不同的。在友誼或愛情裡，倆人肩並肩高舉雙手，探求單一人無法觸及的事物。

——**紀伯倫**《親愛的先知：紀伯倫和瑪麗·哈斯吉爾的情書及她的手記》

You're beautiful, but you're empty...One couldn't die for you. Of course, an ordinary passerby would think my rose looked just like you. But my rose, all on her own, is more important than all of you together, since she's the one I've watered. Since she's the one I put under glass, since she's the one I sheltered behind the screen. Since she's the one for whom I killed the caterpillars (except the two or three butterflies). Since she's the one I listened to when she complained, or when she boasted, or even sometimes when she said nothing at all. Since she's my rose.

——**Antoine de Saint-Exupéry** 1900-1944 : *The Little Prince*

妳們很美，但妳們很空洞……沒有人會為妳們而死。當然，平凡路人可能會認為我的玫瑰看起來就跟妳們一樣。但我的玫瑰，單單是她的存在，就能比妳們都重要，因為她是我親自澆水的。她是我親自放到玻璃罩下的、她是我親自藏到幕遮之後的。我為了她親自殺死毛毛蟲（只留下兩三隻蝴蝶）。我聽她抱怨、聽她自誇、甚至有時候她什麼都不說。因為她是我的玫瑰。

—— 聖修伯里《小王子》

愛恨，鏡像雙生的情感

BOOK OF LOVE

Love conquers all things—except poverty and toothache.

——**Mae West** 1893-1980

愛戰勝一切──除了貧窮與牙痛。

──梅‧蕙絲

He did not care if she was heartless, vicious and vulgar, stupid and grasping, he loved her. He would rather have misery with one than happiness with the other.

——**W. Somerset Maugham** 1874-1965 : *Of Human Bondage*

他才不在意她是否無情、卑劣又粗鄙、愚蠢又貪婪，
他愛她。他寧願跟這個人落得悲慘，也不願與另一
人幸福快樂。

—— **毛姆**《人性枷鎖》

A man enjoys the happiness he feels, a woman the happiness she gives.

——**Pierre Choderlos de Laclos** 1741-1803 : *Les Liaisons Dangereuses*

男人享受他感覺到的快樂，女人享受她給出的快樂。

—— 拉克洛 《危險關係》

It is better to know as little as possible of the defects of the person with whom you are to pass your life.

——**Jane Austen** 1775-1817 : *Pride and Prejudice*

愛恨，鏡像雙生的情感

對於即將共渡一生之人的瑕疵，你知道得越少越好。

——珍・奧斯汀《傲慢與偏見》

If I am pressed to say why I loved him, I feel it can only be explained by replying : Because it was he; because it was me.

——**Montaigne** 1533-1592 : *Essais*

如果我一定得說出我為什麼愛著他，我想唯一能解釋的便是如此回應：因為是他；因為是我。

—— 蒙田《隨筆》

You made me confess the fears that I have. But I will tell you also what I do not fear. I do not fear to be alone or to be spurned for another or to leave whatever I have to leave. And I am not afraid to make a mistake, even a great mistake, a lifelong mistake and perhaps as long as eternity too.

———**James Joyce** 1882-1941 : *A Portrait of the Artist as a Young Man*

你讓我傾吐我所有的恐懼。但我也要告訴你，我並不害怕。我不怕獨處、遭他人唾棄，或是離開我得離開的任何事。我也不怕犯錯，哪怕那是一輩子的滔天大錯，哪怕那可能近乎永恆。

—— 喬伊斯《年輕藝術家的肖像》

愛恨，鏡像雙生的情感

When two people are under the influence of the most violent, most insane, most delusive, and most transient of passions, they are requires to swear that they will remain in that excited, abnormal, and exhausting condition continuously until death do them part.

——**George Bernard Shaw** 1856-1950 : *Getting Married*

當兩人都受到最暴力、最瘋狂、最虛妄且最無常的
激情驅使，他們就得發誓一直處於在那種激動、反
常且耗神的境況當中，直至死亡將他們分開。

── **蕭伯納**《婚姻》

Love takes off the masks we fear we cannot live without and know we cannot live within.

——**James Baldwin** 1924-1987 : *The Fire Next Time*

愛恨，鏡像雙生的情感

愛摘下了我們的面具，那張讓我們唯恐自己不戴就不能過活、同時又深知自己無法戴著過活的面具。

—— **詹姆斯・鮑德溫** 《下一次將是烈火》

You shall be together when the white wings of death scatter your days. Ay, you shall be together even in the silent memory of God. But let there be spaces in your togetherness, And let the winds of the heavens dance between you.

—— **Kahlil Gibran** 1883-1931 : *The Prophet*

在死神的白翼攪擾你們時日之時，你們應該同在。
唉，就算在上帝不語的記憶之中，你們都應該同在。
但為你們的同在騰點空間，讓天堂的風在你們之間
拂舞。

—— 紀伯倫《先知》

Love. The reason I dislike that word is that it means
too much for me, far more than you can understand.

——**Leo Tolstoy** 1828-1910 : *Anna Karenina*

愛恨，鏡像雙生的情感

愛。我之所以討厭這個字，是因為它的意義對我來說太深重了，超乎你所能理解。

——**托爾斯泰**《安娜‧卡列尼娜》

If somebody says 'I love you' to me, I feel as though I had a pistol pointed at my head. What can anybody reply under such conditions but that which the pistol holder requires? 'I love you, too'.

——**Kurt Vonnegut** 1922-2007 : *Wampeters, Foma and Granfalloons*

如果有人對我說「我愛你」，我會覺得好似有把手槍抵著我的頭。任何人在這種狀態下，除了扣下扳機的那句話之外還能回答什麼呢？「我也愛你。」

—— 馮內果 《此心不移》

Dearest, I feel certain that I am going mad again. I feel we can't go through another of those terrible times. And I shan't recover this time. I begin to hear voices, and I can't concentrate. So I am doing what seems the best thing to do. You have given me the greatest possible happiness. You have been in every way all that anyone could be. I don't think two people could have been happier 'til this terrible disease came. I can't fight any longer. I know that I am spoiling your life, that without me you could work. And you will I know. You see I can't even write this properly. I can't read. What I want to say is I owe all the happiness of my life to you. You have been entirely patient with me and incredibly good. I want to say that – everybody knows it. If anybody could have saved me it would have been you. Everything has gone from me but the certainty of your goodness. I can't go on spoiling your life any longer. I don't think two people could have been happier than we have been.

V.

——**Virginia Woolf** 1882-1941 : *Suicide note to Leonard*

我最親愛的，我想我真的又要瘋了。我想我們無法再攜手走過另一段恐怖的時光了。而我這次不會好起來了。我開始害怕聲音、無法專注。所以我做了一個看來最好的決定。你給過我無比的幸福，你已為我付出任何人能為我付出的所有一切。我不認為還有哪兩個人能比我們更開心──直到這個可怕的疾病襲來。我沒辦法繼續搏鬥下去了。我知道自己正在毀掉你的生活，要是沒有我，你就能專注工作。你會的，我知道。你看，我甚至連好好把它寫下來都沒辦法。我不能閱讀。我想說的是，我此生的幸福都虧欠於你。你對我付出了全然的耐性與難以置信的溫柔。我想說出來──儘管大家都知道。如果還有誰能拯救我的話，那將會是你。所有事物都在棄我而去，唯獨你的溫柔依舊。我不能這麼繼續毀掉你的人生。我不覺得還有人能比我們幸福。

V。

── 吳爾芙，投河自盡前留給丈夫里歐納德的信

To love is to suffer and there can be no love otherwise.

—— **Fyodor Dostoyevsky** 1821-1881 : *Notes from Underground*

愛恨，鏡像雙生的情感

愛就是受苦，除此之外別無可能。

──杜斯妥耶夫斯基《地下室手記》

愛恨，鏡像雙生的情感

III

幸福的海市蜃樓

The heart was made to be broken.

——**Oscar Wilde** 1854-1900 : *De Profundis*

愛恨，鏡像雙生的情感

心是用來碎的。

―― 王爾德《深淵書簡》

BOOK OF LOVE

It seemed to them that fate itself had meant them for one another, and they could not understand why he had a wife and she a husband; and it was as though they were a pair of birds of passage, caught and forced to live in a different cages.

——**Anton Chekhov** 1860-1904 : *The Lady with the Dog*

命運看來在他們兩人面前都呈現為彼此，他們都無
法了解，為什麼他有一個妻子、而她又有一個丈夫；
好像他們是一對被擒獲的候鳥，受迫在不同的籠子
裡生活。

—— 契訶夫《帶狗的女士》

愛恨，鏡像雙生的情感

Lovers' vows do not reach the ears of the gods.

——**Callimachus** 305-240 BC : *Epigrams*

愛恨，鏡像雙生的情感

戀人的誓言並未抵達諸神的耳裡。

—— 卡利馬科斯《語錄》

When I was in the military, they gave me a medal for killing two men and a discharge for loving one.

──**Leonard Matlovich** 1943-1988 : *Tombstone Epitaph*

愛恨，鏡像雙生的情感

我還在軍中時，因為殺了兩個男人而獲頒勳章，卻因為愛上一個男人而遭到革職。

—— 美國同志軍人馬特洛維奇之墓碑文

Love ceases to be a pleasure, when it ceases to be a secret.

——**Aphra Behn** 1640-1689 : *The Lover's Watch*

愛恨,鏡像雙生的情感

當愛不再是祕密，它就不再是喜悅。

—— 阿芙拉・貝恩《戀人的注視》

Immature love says: I love you because I need you.

Mature love says: I need you because I love you.

──**Erich Fromm** 1900-1980 : *The Art of Loving*

不成熟的愛會說：我愛你，因為我需要你。

成熟的愛會說：我需要你，因為我愛你。

── 弗洛姆 《愛的藝術》

People insist on confusing marriage and love on the one hand, and love and happiness on the other. But they have nothing in common. That is why, the absence of love being more frequent than love, there are happy marriage.

——**Albert Camus** 1913-1960 : *Carnets*

人們不斷混淆婚姻與愛情，同時又不斷混淆愛情與
幸福。但這三者之間其實毫無共通之處。所以當愛
時常缺席，我們就有了快樂的婚姻。

—— 卡繆《札記》

BOOK OF LOVE

The one charm of marriage is that it makes a life of deception absolutely necessary for both parties.

———**Oscar Wilde** 1854-1900 : *The Picture of Dorian Gray*

愛恨，鏡像雙生的情感

婚姻的一個迷人之處，在於它創造了一種生活，那是一場對兩造而言都絕對必要的騙局。

—— 王爾德《格雷的畫像》

The test of a man or woman's breeding is how they
behave in a quarrel.

——**George Bernard Shaw** 1856-1950 : *The Philanderer*

男人與女人在教養上的測試，就是他們在口角當中
如何表現。

—— **蕭伯納**《登徒子》

The more one judges, the less one loves.

—— **Honoré de Balzac** 1799-1850 : *Physiologie Du Mariage*

挑剔得愈多，愛得愈少。

──**巴爾札克**《婚姻生理學》

Those who have courage to love should have courage to suffer.

——**Anthony Trollope** 1815-1882 : *The Bertrams*

有膽量去愛的人也必須有膽量受苦。

——安東尼·特洛勒普《貝川一家》

愛恨，鏡像雙生的情感

Do you think, because I am poor, obscure, plain and little, I am soulless and heartless? You think wrong! — I have as much soul as you, — and full as much heart! And if God had gifted me with some beauty and much wealth, I should have made it as hard for you to leave me, as it is now for me to leave you!

——**Charlotte Brontë** 1816-1855 : *Jane Eyre*

難道你以為，因為我貧寒、低微、無名而渺小，我
就沒有靈魂也沒有心嗎？你大錯特錯！—— 我有跟
你相同的靈魂 —— 也裝著一顆跟你一樣的心！如果
上天賦予我些許美貌與更多財富，我早就讓你對我
欲罷不能了，就像我現在對你欲罷不能一樣。

—— 夏綠蒂・勃朗特《簡愛》

A kiss is a lovely trick designed by nature to stop speech when words become superfluous.

——**Ingrid Bergman** 1915-1982

吻是自然設計的迷人技倆，能在字詞流於膚淺時擋下一切話語。

—— 英格麗褒曼

The most happy marriage I can picture or imagine to myself would be the union of a deaf man to a blind woman.

——**Samuel Taylor Coleridge** 1772-1834

我能想像的最幸福婚姻，會是聾男與盲女的結合。

—— 柯立芝

Marrying a man is like buying something you have been admiring for a long time in a shop window. You may love it when you get it home, but it doesn't always go with everything else in the house.

——**Jean Kerr** 1922-2003 : *The Snake Has All the Lines*

嫁給一個男人就像終於買下一件你在櫥窗裡看了很久的東西。剛買回家時你可能還愛著他，但他不會一直和屋裡的每樣東西都相襯。

—— **琴‧凱爾** 《每句台詞都是蛇的》

I really don't see anything romantic in proposing. It is very romantic to be in love. But there is nothing romantic about a definite proposal. Why, one may be accepted. One usually is, I believe. Then the excitement is all over. The very essence of romance is uncertainty. If ever I get married, I'll certainly try to forget the fact.

——**Oscar Wilde** 1854-1900 : *The Importance of Being Earnest*

我真心不懂求婚有什麼浪漫可言。談戀愛是浪漫的，但一場明確的求婚可說是毫不浪漫。為什麼呢？被求婚者可能會接受 —— 我相信通常會接受。然後，激情就結束了。浪漫的精髓在於不確定性。就算我結婚了，肯定也會設法忘記這件事。

—— 王爾德《不可兒戲》

It's afterwards you realize that the feeling of happiness you had with a man didn't necessarily prove that you loved him.

——**Marguerite Duras** 1914-1996 : *Practicalities*

你得在事後才能理解，跟一個男人在一起的快樂感
受並不必然保證你愛他。

—— 莒哈絲《日常瑣碎》

Though jealousy be produced by love, as ashes are by fire, yet jealousy extinguishes love as ashes smothers the flame.

——**Marguerite d'Angoulême** 1492-1549 : *The Heptameron*

儘管嫉妒由愛所生，猶如灰燼自火而出，然而嫉妒
會撲滅愛情，猶如灰燼悶熄焰火。

—— 瑪格麗特・德・昂古萊姆《七日談》

Love frequently dies of time alone — much more frequently of displacement.

——**Thomas Hardy** 1840-1928 : *A Pair of Blue Eyes*

愛恨，鏡像雙生的情感

愛經常只是日子一久就死絕 —— 但更常是因為不合時宜。

—— 湯瑪士・哈代《一雙碧眼》

Adultery introduces some energy into an otherwise dead marriage.

——**Marcel Proust** 1871-1922 : *À La Recherche du Temps Perdu*

暗通款曲為註定一死的婚姻注入了能量。

—— **普魯斯特**《追憶似水年華》

The moment I swear to love a woman, a certain woman, all my life, that moment I begin to hate her.

——**D.H. Lawrence** 1885-1930 : *'The Mess of Love'*

愛恨，鏡像雙生的情感

當我誓言愛上一個女人、終其一生只愛一個特定的
女人──從那刻起，我便開始恨她。

──D.H. 勞倫斯〈大量的愛〉

Plasir d'amour ne dure qu'un moment,
Chagrin d'amour dure toute la vie.

——**Jean-Pierre Claris de Florian** 1755-1794 : *Célestine*

愛的喜樂僅存一時，

愛的憂苦綿延一世。

—— 尚-皮耶‧克拉里斯‧德弗羅里昂《賽勒絲汀》

The chains of marriage are so heavy that it takes two to bear them, and sometimes three.

——**Alexander Dumas** 1802-1870

婚姻的枷鎖如此沈重，需要兩人方能共同背負 ——
不過偶爾需要三人。

—— 大仲馬

Jealousy is never satisfied with anything short of an omniscience that would detect the subtlest fold of the heart.

——**George Eliot** 1819-1880 : *The Mill on the Floss*

嫉妒永遠不會因為任何缺乏某種全知的事物而平歇，
那種全知能感受心上每道細微摺痕。

—— **喬治・艾略特** *《弗洛斯河上的磨坊》*

You know, of course, that the Tasmanians, who never
committed adultery, are now extinct.

———**W. Somerset Maugham** 1874-1965 : *The Bread-Winner*

你知道，當然了，塔斯馬尼亞人從不通姦，他們現在絕跡了。

——**毛姆**《養家活口的人》

For man, infidelity is not inconstancy.

——**Pierre Choderlos de Laclos** 1741-1803 : *Les Liaisons Dangereuses*

對男人而言，不忠並非缺乏定性。

　　──拉克洛《危險關係》

There is no infidelity when there has been no love.

———**Honoré de Balzac** 1799-1850 : *Letter to Madame Hanska*

無愛則無所謂不忠。

——巴爾札克，致漢絲卡夫人書信

Yet each man kills the thing he loves
By each let this be heard
Some do it with a bitter look
Some with a flattering word
The coward does it with a kiss
The brave man with a sword

——**Oscar Wilde** 1854-1900 : *The Ballad Of Reading Gaol*

而每個人殺死他們所愛

且讓我們娓娓道來

有人滿臉愁苦

有人一嘴諂媚

懦弱之徒只以一個吻

勇敢之人提起一把劍

　　—— 王爾德《瑞丁監獄之歌》

When a man steal your wife, there is no better revenge than to let him keep her.

——**Sacha Guitry** 1885-1957 : *Elles et Toi*

愛恨，鏡像雙生的情感

當一個男人偷了你的妻子，最好的復仇方式就是讓他留著她。

—— 沙夏‧吉特里《她與你》

Those have most power to hurt us that we love.

——**Francis Beaumont** 1584-1616 : *The Maid's Tragedy*

那些最有能力傷害我們的都是我們所愛的。

—— **法蘭西斯・波蒙** 《女僕的悲劇》

Sex is the consolation you have when you can't have
love

——**Gabriel García Márquez** 1927-2014

性是愛不可得時的慰藉。

—— 馬奎斯

It is not a lack of love, but a lack of friendship that makes unhappy marriages.

——**Friedrich Nietzsche** 1844-1900

不快樂的婚姻缺乏的並非愛情，而是友誼。

—— 尼采

There are some meannesses which are too mean even
for man—woman, lovely woman alone, can venture to
commit them.

——**William Makepeace Thackeray** 1811-1863 : *A Shabby
Genteel Story*

有些歹毒之事連對男人而言都太過歹毒 —— 女人，
只有可愛的女人，能夠大膽犯下惡行。

—— 薩克萊《一個死要面子的故事》

Anyone who hasn't experienced the ecstasy of betrayal knows nothing about ecstasy at all.

——**Jean Genet** 1910-1986 : *Prisoner of Love*

愛恨，鏡像雙生的情感

任何人若沒體驗過背叛帶來的狂喜，就對狂喜一無所知。

—— 尚・惹內《愛的囚徒》

Reading someone else's newspaper is like sleeping with someone else's wife. Nothing seems to be precisely in the right place, and when you find what you are looking for, it is not clear then how to respond to it.

———**Malcolm Bradbury** 1932-2000 : *Stepping Westward*

讀別人的報紙就像睡別人的老婆。一眼望去沒有任何人事物是精準地待在正確的位置上的，而當你終於找到想看的東西之後，卻又不太明白該如何應對。

—— 馬爾科姆‧布雷德伯里《西行》

Anger and jealousy can no more bear to lose sight of their objects than love.

———**George Eliot** 1819-1880 : *The Mill on the Floss*

憤怒與嫉妒在愛消失於它們視野中時最讓人無法承
受。

—— 喬治・艾略特 《弗洛斯河上的磨坊》

It was very good of God to let Carlyle and Mrs. Carlyle marry one another and so make only two people miserable instead of four.

——**Samuel Butler** 1835-1902 : *Letter to Miss E.M.A. Savage*

上帝相當仁慈，讓卡利爾夫婦結縭；如此一來將只
有兩人活得悽慘落魄，而非四人。

——山繆・巴特勒，致 E.M.A. 薩瓦吉小姐書信

BOOK OF LOVE

A woman may very well form a friendship with a man, but for this to endure, it must be assisted by a little physical antipathy.

——**Friedrich Nietzsche** 1844-1900 : *Human, All Too Human*

女人也能跟男人建立良好友誼，但此情若要長久，
必得借助一點肉體上的反感。

—— 尼采 《人性的，太人性的》

Friendship is a disinterested commerce between equals; love, an abject intercourse between tyrants and slaves.

——**Oliver Goldsmith** 1728-1774 : *The Good–Natured Man*

愛恨，鏡像雙生的情感

友誼是平起兩造之間的公平交易；愛情則是暴君奴
隸之間的下賤來往。

──奧利弗・戈德史密斯《人性本善》

A woman can become a man's friend only in the following stages—first an acquaintance, next a mistress, and only then a firend.

—**Anton Chekhov** 1860-1904 : *Uncle Vanya*

女人只能在通過如下階段後才能成為男人的朋友：
一開始是個相識、再來是個女伴，而接下來就只是
個朋友。

—— **契訶夫** 《凡尼亞舅舅》

A man can be happy with any woman as long as he
does not love her.

—— **Oscar Wilde** 1854-1900 : *The Picture of Dorian Gray*

一個男人可以跟隨便一個女人幸福美滿 —— 只要不
愛上她。

—— 王爾德《格雷的畫像》

It is very hard to be in love with someone who no longer loves you, but it is far worse to be loved by someone with whom you are no longer in love.

——**Georges Courteline** 1858-1929 : *La Philosophie de Georges Courteline*

愛上不再愛你的人相當辛苦，但被你已再無感情的人所愛卻是遠遠地更糟。

—— **喬治・庫特林**《喬治・庫特林的人生哲學》

It is the property of love to make us at once more distrustful and more credulous, to make us suspect the loved one, more readily than we should suspect anyone else, and be convinced more easily by her denials.

——**Marcel Proust** 1871-1922 : *À La Recherche du Temps Perdu*

愛的屬性讓我們更加多疑，同時卻也更容易受騙，它讓我們更會去質疑自己所愛，比質疑他人還更欣然爽快，而又更輕易地被她的否認給說服。

—— 普魯斯特《追憶似水年華》

BOOK OF LOVE

愛恨，鏡像雙生的情感

245

Nobody sees anybody truly but all through the flaws of their own egos. That is the way we all see each other in life. Vanity, fear, desire, competition—all such distortions within our own egos—condition our vision of those in relation to us. Add to those distortions to our own egos the corresponding distortions in the egos of others, and you see how cloudy the glass must become through which we look at each other. That's how it is in all living relationships except when there is that rare case of two people who love intensely enough to burn through all those layers of opacity and see each other's naked hearts.

——**Tennessee Williams** 1911-1983 : *Letter to Elia Kazan*

沒有人能真正看到他人全貌，惟有透過自我缺陷。那便是我們終其一生看待彼此的方式。虛榮、恐懼、欲望、競爭——我們內在自我當中的所有扭曲——限制了我們看待旁人的眼光。當我們把自我扭曲疊加到他人對應的缺陷上，你會明白，我們觀看彼此的透鏡何其模糊。這就是所有人類自然關係的道理——除了在罕見例子當中，兩個人愛得夠熾烈，足以燒盡層層掩翳，看見對方赤裸的心。

——田納西·威廉斯，致導演伊力·卡山書信

What is insane about love is that one wishes to precipitate and to lose the days of waiting. Thus one desires to approach the end. So by one of its characteristics love coincides with death.

——**Albert Camus** 1913-1960 : *Diary,* April 1950

關於愛，最瘋狂的是一個人希望能加速並拋棄等待的那些日子。如此一來，人就渴望迎向結局。所以，對如此性格的人來說，愛恰巧就是死。

——卡繆，日記，一九五〇年四月

Ultimately, it is the desire, not the desired, that we love.

——**Friedrich Nietzsche** 1844-1900

愛恨，鏡像雙生的情感

我們愛的，終究是欲望本身，而非欲望的對象。

——尼采

IV

如夢初醒

Stronger than lover's love is lover's hate. Incurable, in each, the wounds they make.

——**Euripides** 480-406 BC : *Medea*

愛恨，鏡像雙生的情感

比戀人的愛還強大的是戀人的恨。他們為彼此留下
的傷痕無藥可救。

—— **歐里庇得斯**《米蒂亞》

There is no love sincerer than the love of food.

——**George Bernard Shaw** 1856-1950 : *Man and Superman*

愛恨，鏡像雙生的情感

世間真情真不過對食物的愛。

—— **蕭伯納**《人與超人》

愛恨，鏡像雙生的情感

BOOK OF LOVE

Love is a sickness full of woes,

All remedies refusing;

A plant that with most cutting grows,

Most barren with best using.

——**Samuel Daniel** 1563-1619 : *'Love'*

愛恨，鏡像雙生的情感

愛是一場苦難滿溢的病，
抗拒所有解藥；
愛是一片飽受墾伐的林，
愈善用則不毛。

——山繆・丹尼爾〈愛〉

Love in action is a harsh and dreadful thing compared to love in dreams.

——**Fyodor Dostoyevsky** 1821-1881 : *The Brothers Karamazov*

愛恨，鏡像雙生的情感

跟夢想裡的愛相較，實際的愛是一種嚴苛又駭人的
東西。

—— **杜斯妥耶夫斯基**《卡拉馬佐夫兄弟們》

To love at all is to be vulnerable. Love anything and your heart will be wrung and possibly broken. If you want to make sure of keeping it intact you must give it to no one, not even an animal. Wrap it carefully round with hobbies and little luxuries; avoid all entanglements. Lock it up safe in the casket or coffin of your selfishness. But in that casket, safe, dark, motionless, airless, it will change. It will not be broken; it will become unbreakable, impenetrable, irredeemable. To love is to be vulnerable.

——**C.S. Lewis** 1898-1963 : *The Four Loves*

去愛，說到底就是變得脆弱。愛撏絞你的心，還可能將之擊碎。若要確保心的完整，就絕對不能將它交給任何人 —— 連動物都不行。仔細地用小確幸包裹它，迴避一切纏綿糾葛。將它深鎖在你自私的箱匣棺柩之內。但在那安全、黑暗、死寂、窒息的小箱中，心會產生變化。它不會再被擊碎；它堅固不摧、無法滲透、難以撼搖。而愛就是變得脆弱。

—— C.S. 路易士《四種愛》

There should be an invention that bottles up a memory like a perfume, and it never faded, never got stale, and whenever I wanted to I could uncork the bottle, and live the memory all over again.

——**Daphne Du Maurier** 1907-1989 : *Rebecca*

應該要發明這麼一種裝置，把回憶像香水一般裝入瓶中，永不褪色、永不走味，只要我高興就拔開瓶塞，讓整段記憶重新活過一次。

──戴芙妮・杜・莫里哀《蝴蝶夢》

Love is so short, forgetting is so long.

———**Pablo Neruda** 1904-1973 : *Love: Ten Poems*

愛恨，鏡像雙生的情感

相愛何其短暫，遺忘又何其漫長。

—— **聶魯達**《十首情詩》

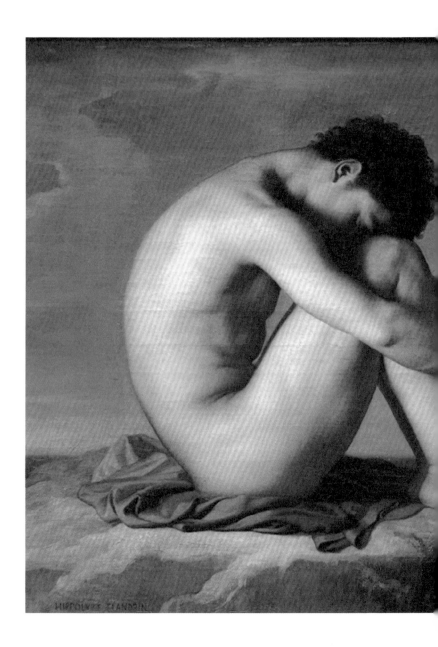

愛恨，鏡像雙生的情感

BOOK OF LOVE

If you love something so much let it go. If it comes back it was meant to be; if it doesn't it never was.

——**Albert Schweitzer** 1875-1965

如果你深愛著某事，那就讓它去吧。如果它回頭，它註定要回頭；如果它不，它也從來都不。

—— 史懷哲

The saddest thing about love, Joe, is that not only the love cannot last forever, but even the heartbreak is soon forgotten.

——**William Faulkner** 1897-1952 : *Soldier's Pay*

愛最讓人傷心的一點就是，喬，愛不僅無法永垂不朽，就連心碎也都過眼即忘。

──威廉・福克納《士兵的報酬》

I love you; and perhaps I love you still,
The flame, perhaps, is not extinguished; yet
It burns so quietly within my soul,
No longer should you feel distressed by it.

——**Alexander Pushkin** 1799-1837 : *'I love You'*

愛恨，鏡像雙生的情感

我愛你；或許我仍愛著你，
愛火或許尚未滅跡；然而
它默默在我靈魂深處燃燒，
你不應繼續為此苦惱。

—— 普希金〈我愛你〉

Confession is not betrayal. What you say or do doesn't matter; only feelings matter. If they could make me stop loving you-that would be the real betrayal.

——**George Orwell** 1903-1950 : *1984*

坦白不是背叛。你說的跟做的都不重要；重要的只
有感受。如果這些感受會讓我不再愛你，那才是真
正的背叛。

—— **喬治・歐威爾**《一九八四》

Silently and hopelessly I loved you,
At times too jealousy and at times too shy.
God grant you find another who will love you
As tenderly and truthfully as I.

——**Alexander Pushkin** 1799-1837 : *'I love You'*

靜默而無望地，我曾愛你，
偶爾過於嫉妒，偶爾過於羞赧。
願神許諾你尋得另一人愛你，
願他溫柔而信實如我。

—— 普希金〈我愛你〉

愛恨，鏡像雙生的情感

And the best and the worst of this is

That neither is most to blame,

If you have forgotten my kisses

And I have forgotten your name.

——**Algernon Charles Swinburne** 1837-1909 : *'An Interlude'*

最好與最壞的都是

這兩者皆毋需多加責難，

不論是你忘了我的吻

或是我忘了你的名。

—— 史雲朋〈插曲〉

I think it is all a matter of love; the more you love a
memory the stronger and stranger it becomes

——**Vladimir Nabokov** 1899-1977

愛恨，鏡像雙生的情感

我想一切都是愛；你越愛一段記憶，它就變得越強大、越不可思議。

──納博科夫

A man who has not passed through the inferno of his passions has never overcome them.

——**Carl Jung** 1875-1961 : *Memoires, Dreams, Reflections*

沒有經歷過激情的地獄之人永遠無法超克激情。

—— **榮格**《回憶、夢境、反思》

Body, remember not only how much you were loved,
not only the beds on which you lay,
but also those desires which for you
plainly glowed in the eyes,
and trembled in the voice.

——**Constantine Cavafy** 1863-1933 : *Body Remember*

身體啊，不要只記得自己曾經多麼被愛，

不要只記得你躺過的那些床褥，

也要記得那些向你奉上的欲望——

在凝視你的眼裡發出微光、

在他們的聲音中顫抖。

—— 康斯坦丁・卡瓦菲〈身體請記得〉

BOOK OF LOVE

Parting is all we know of heaven,
And all we need of hell.

——**Emily Dickinson** 1830-1886 : ' *My life closed twice before its*
close'

離別是我們對天堂僅知的一切，

從而我們都需要地獄。

—— 艾蜜莉·狄金生 〈我的生命在結束之前曾闔上兩次〉

There are two basic motivating forces: fear and love. When we are afraid, we pull back from life. When we are in love, we open to all that life has to offer with passion, excitement, and acceptance. We need to learn to love ourselves first, in all our glory and our imperfections. If we cannot love ourselves, we cannot fully open to our ability to love others or our potential to create. Evolution and all hopes for a better world rest in the fearlessness and open-hearted vision of people who embrace life.

——**John Lennon** 1940-1980

人類有兩種基本動能：恐懼與愛。當我們害怕，我們會從生活中退縮。當我們愛，我們便懷抱熱情、興奮與寬容，向生命所提供的一切敞開自我。我們首先得學會自愛，擁抱自己的一切榮耀與所有缺憾。若不能自愛，我們就無法完全開啟我們的愛人能力或是創造潛能。進化與朝向更好世界的所有想望，都源於擁抱生命者的無所畏懼與開放視野。

——約翰·藍儂

The only unnatural sex act is that which you cannot perform.

——**Alfred Kinsey** : in *Time* January 1966

唯一不自然的性行為是你做不來的那些。

──金賽，一九六六年一月刊於《時代》雜誌

It is better to be hated for what you are than to be loved for what you are not.

———**André Gide** 1869-1951 : *Autumn Leaves*

被他人恨自己所是，好過被愛自己所不是。

──紀德《秋葉》

You can love a person dear to you with a human love,
but an enemy can only be loved with divine love.

——**Leo Tolstoy** 1828-1910 : *War and Peace*

你能夠以凡人之愛去愛一個親近的人，但你只能以神聖之愛去愛一個敵人。

── **托爾斯泰** 《戰爭與和平》

Better by far you should forget and smile
Than that you should remember and be sad.

——**Christina Rossetti** 1830-1894 : *'Remember'*

左思右想，你該遺忘一切並微笑
這怎麼都好過記得全部而悲傷。

──克莉斯緹娜・羅塞蒂〈記得〉

It's so curious: one can resist tears and 'behave' very well in the hardest hours of grief. But then someone makes you a friendly sign behind a window, or one notices that a flower that was in bud only yesterday has suddenly blossomed, or a letter slips from a drawer...and everything collapses.

——**Colette** 1873-1954

這個現象很奇妙：一個人能夠在哀悼的最艱苦之際抗拒淚水、舉止得宜。但只要有人從窗戶後頭給你一個友善的暗示、注意到一朵昨日的蓓蕾突然綻放，或只是一封滑出抽屜的信……一切就崩潰了。

──柯蕾特

A crowd is not company, and faces are but a gallery of pictures, and talk but a tinkling cymbal, where there is no love.

———**Francis Bacon** 1561-1626 : *Essays 'Of Friendship'*

若是沒有愛，人群不會是陪伴，張張臉孔也不過是
藝廊圖畫，而交談就只是銅鈸擦響。

—— 培根《論友誼》

Sex is more exciting on the screen and between the pages than between the sheets.

——**Andy Warhol** 1928-1987 : *Philosophy of Andy Warhol*

愛恨，鏡像雙生的情感

性在螢幕上與書頁間，都比在床單裡更令人興奮。

──**安迪‧沃荷**《安迪‧沃荷的人生哲學》

The lovely thing about being forty is that you can appreciate twenty-five-yeard old men more.

——**Collen McCullough** 1937-2015

年近四十的好處，就是讓你更能欣賞二十五歲的男人。

—— 柯琳‧馬嘉露

'Bed,' as the Italian proverb succinctly puts it, ' is the poor man's opera.'

——**Aldous Huxley** 1894-1963 : *Heaven and Hell*

愛恨，鏡像雙生的情感

「床，」如同義大利俗諺的簡潔描述，「是窮人的歌劇院。」

—— **赫胥黎**《天堂與地獄》

Love, like fire, cannot survive without continual movement, and it ceases to live as soon as it ceases to hope or fear.

——**Duc de la Rochefoucauld** 1613-1680 : *Maximes*

愛情如火焰，若無持續運動則無法存活，而一旦停止希望或有所畏懼，愛便終止生命。

──拉羅什福柯《人性箴言》

愛恨，鏡像雙生的情感

BOOK OF LOVE

What is hell? I maintain that it is the suffering of being unable to love.

———**Fyodor Dostoyevsky** 1821-1881 : *The Brothers Karamazov*

何謂地獄？我斷言那便是無能去愛的折磨。

—— 杜斯妥耶夫斯基《卡拉馬佐夫兄弟們》

A man who loves like a woman becomes a slave; but a woman who loves like a woman becomes a more perfect woman.

——**Friedrich Nietzsche** 1844-1900 : *The Gay Science*

一個男人愛得像個女人，他就淪落為奴隸；但一個
女人愛得像個女人，她便提昇為更完美的女人。

──尼采《愉快的科學》

In itself, homosexuality is as limiting as heterosexuality: the ideal should be to be capable of loving a woman or a man; either, a human being, without feeling fear, restraint, or obligation.

——**Simone de Beauvoir** 1908-1986

就本身而論，同性戀與異性戀同樣受限：理想而言，一個人應該要能愛上一個男人或女人 —— *毋*寧說，任一個人類 —— 而不必感受到畏懼、限制或受義務所累。

—— 西蒙・波娃

When love has fused and mingled two beings in a sacred and angelic unity, the secret of life has been discovered so far as they are concerned; they are no longer anything more than the two boundaries of the same destiny; they are no longer anything but the two wings of the same spirit. Love, soar.

——**Victor Hugo** 1802-1885 : *Les Misérables*

當愛將兩個生命溶混成神聖的共同體，雙方一生的奧祕就被揭開了；他們今後就是相同命運的兩道邊界、一脈精神的兩隻翅膀。相愛，翱翔。

—— 雨果《悲慘世界》

It may be important to great thinkers to examine the world, to explain and despise it. But I think it is only important to love the world, not to despise it, not for us to hate each other, but to be able to regard the world and ourselves and all beings with love, admiration and respect.

——**Hermann Hesse** 1877-1962 : *Siddhartha*

對偉大思想者來說，檢驗、解釋與鄙棄這個世界或許很重要。但我想唯有愛這個世界才重要，不是鄙棄它，不是讓我們彼此憎恨，而是能抱持著愛、欣賞與敬意來看待這個世界與我們自己，以及所有存在。

——**赫曼・赫塞**《流浪者之歌》

愛恨，鏡像雙生的情感

ILLUSTRATIONS

愛恨，鏡像雙生的情感

作者／毛姆、雨果、珍・奧斯汀……等人
譯者／王凌緯

總編輯／富察
主題策畫／林家任
執行編輯／林子揚、林家任
行銷／蔡慧華、趙凰佑

排版／宸遠彩藝
設計／井十二設計研究室

社長／郭重興
發行人／曾大福
出版發行／八旗文化・遠足文化事業股份有限公司
地址／新北市新店區民權路 108-2 號 9 樓
電話／02.2218.1417
傳真／02.8667.1065
客服專線／0800.221.029
信箱／gusa0601@gmail.com

法律顧問／華洋法律事務所 蘇文生律師
印刷／通南彩色印刷股份有限公司
出版日期／2017 年 07 月／初版一刷
定價／新台幣 360 元

愛恨，鏡像雙生的情感
毛姆等著；王凌緯譯
初版・新北市
八旗文化，遠足文化，2017.07
336 面；13 × 21 公分
中英對照
ISBN 978-986-94865-4-5（平裝）

813.6
106008024